You're In Love, Charlie Brown

You're In LOVE, Charlie Brown

by Charles M. Schulz

THE WORLD PUBLISHING COMPANY
CLEVELAND AND NEW YORK

Published by The World Publishing Company
2231 West 110th Street, Cleveland, Ohio 44102
Published simultaneously in Canada by Nelson, Foster & Scott Ltd.

First Edition

Copyright © 1968 by United Feature Syndicate, Inc.
Produced in association with
Lee Mendelson–Bill Melendez TV Production

Illustrations from the Lee Mendelson–Bill Melendez
television production "You're In Love, Charlie Brown."

Library of Congress Catalog Card Number: 67–24484

PRINTED IN THE UNITED STATES OF AMERICA

You're In Love, Charlie Brown

Love? How could anyone possibly imagine that a funny little kid like Charlie Brown could be in love? Why, Charlie Brown usually spends most of his time complaining that he doesn't even have any friends. How could someone like that be in love? Well, Linus had listened to Charlie Brown tell how strange he had been feeling lately—how he just didn't seem to know what he was doing, and things like that—and Linus was a shrewd judge of character. He also was quite observant.

He had seen Charlie Brown looking at that pretty
little red-haired girl who rode the bus to school,
and so he was able to remark very confidently,

"I know what your trouble is. You're in love, Charlie Brown!"

Of course, it's one thing to like someone in your class, but it's another matter completely to find out if that person likes you. Charlie Brown tried the old flower method, and as he plucked each petal from a nice white flower, he recited those words that were supposed to give him his answer: "She loves me, she loves me not, she loves me, she loves me not." He never really finished, however, for Linus broke in with a statement that sort of deflated the whole business.

"It is difficult for me to believe that a flower could ever have the gift of prophecy!"

When they got into school, Charlie Brown decided that he'd write a note to the little red-haired girl and try to give it to her sometime during the day. Just as he was writing the note, the teacher called upon him to recite.

He had to take a stack of papers to the front of the class, and in his nervousness he dropped them all over the floor. Then, after considerable fumbling about, he began to read his report.

"Dear little red-haired girl—How I have longed to meet you!"
The class roared with laughter. Poor Charlie Brown. He had read the wrong paper. There's nothing like having the whole class laugh at you to make you wish you had been born a million years ago.

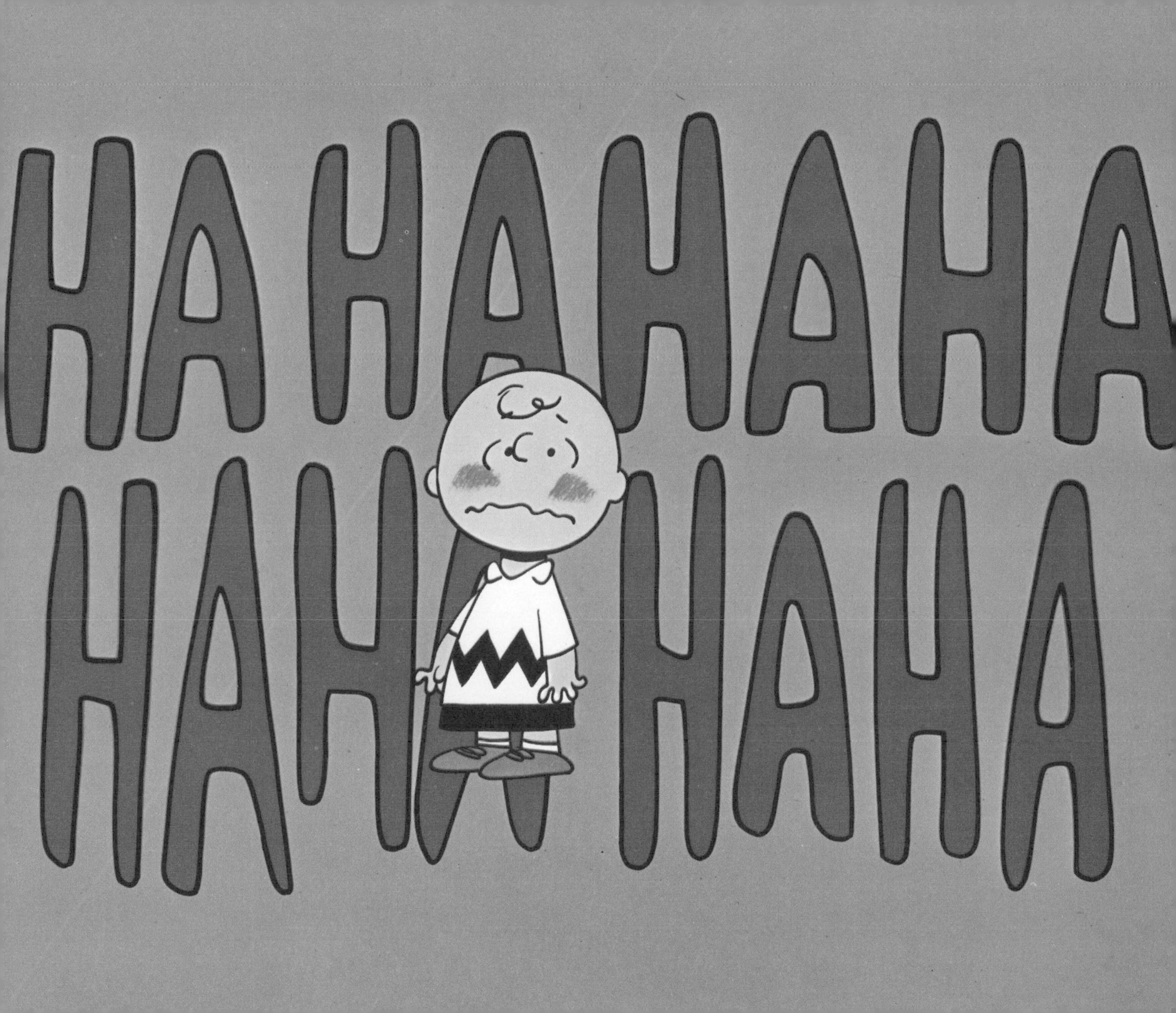
HAHAHAHAHA
HAHAHAHA

During the lunch hour, Charlie Brown felt even worse. All the other kids ran and played together,

but he sat alone on a bench. He longed to be able to go over to the little red-haired girl and ask her to eat lunch with him, but he simply didn't have the nerve. That is a difficult thing to do if you feel you are not much of a person and if you are afraid of being laughed at.

When lunch period was over, Charlie Brown realized what a spot he was in. This day was half over and tomorrow would be the last day of school. Once school was out, he would have to wait until summer was over to see her again. He knew he had to meet her soon or wait until fall. "Wait until fall?" That would be impossible! How could anyone who was so fascinated by someone ever wait for three whole months before he could see her again? At one time during the afternoon he went over to the pencil sharpener where he thought he might talk to her, but he got nervous again and ended up sharpening his ball-point pen by mistake.

By the time he went to bed that night, Charlie Brown knew what he had to do. Tomorrow was the last day of school, and it would be only a half-day session. Therefore, he would have to meet the little red-haired girl at the school bus. He set his alarm for four o'clock just to make sure that he would be there in time.

When the alarm went off at four o'clock in the morning, Charlie Brown felt like he had been stepped on by an elephant.

His eyes were barely open as he went outside.

It was still dark, of course, when he arrived at the bus stop,

and it wasn't long before he found he simply could not stay awake.

When the bus finally came about four hours later, Charlie Brown was sound asleep.

The roar of the bus pulling away from the curb awakened him. It was too late. He ran down the street trying to catch it, but it was no use.

This meant that not only was he not going to get to school early—he wasn't going to be on time at all!

Charlie Brown climbed over the school fence, and tried to open the doors quietly, but they clacked so hard you could hear them all over and the noise echoed down the empty halls.

He crawled along the floor, and was just beside his desk when the teacher saw him. Now he had to explain why he was late, and also go right up to the chalkboard and work out one of the math problems that had been assigned.

"Just watch this, Linus," he whispered. "I'll whip through this problem like a human computer and really impress that little red-haired girl!"

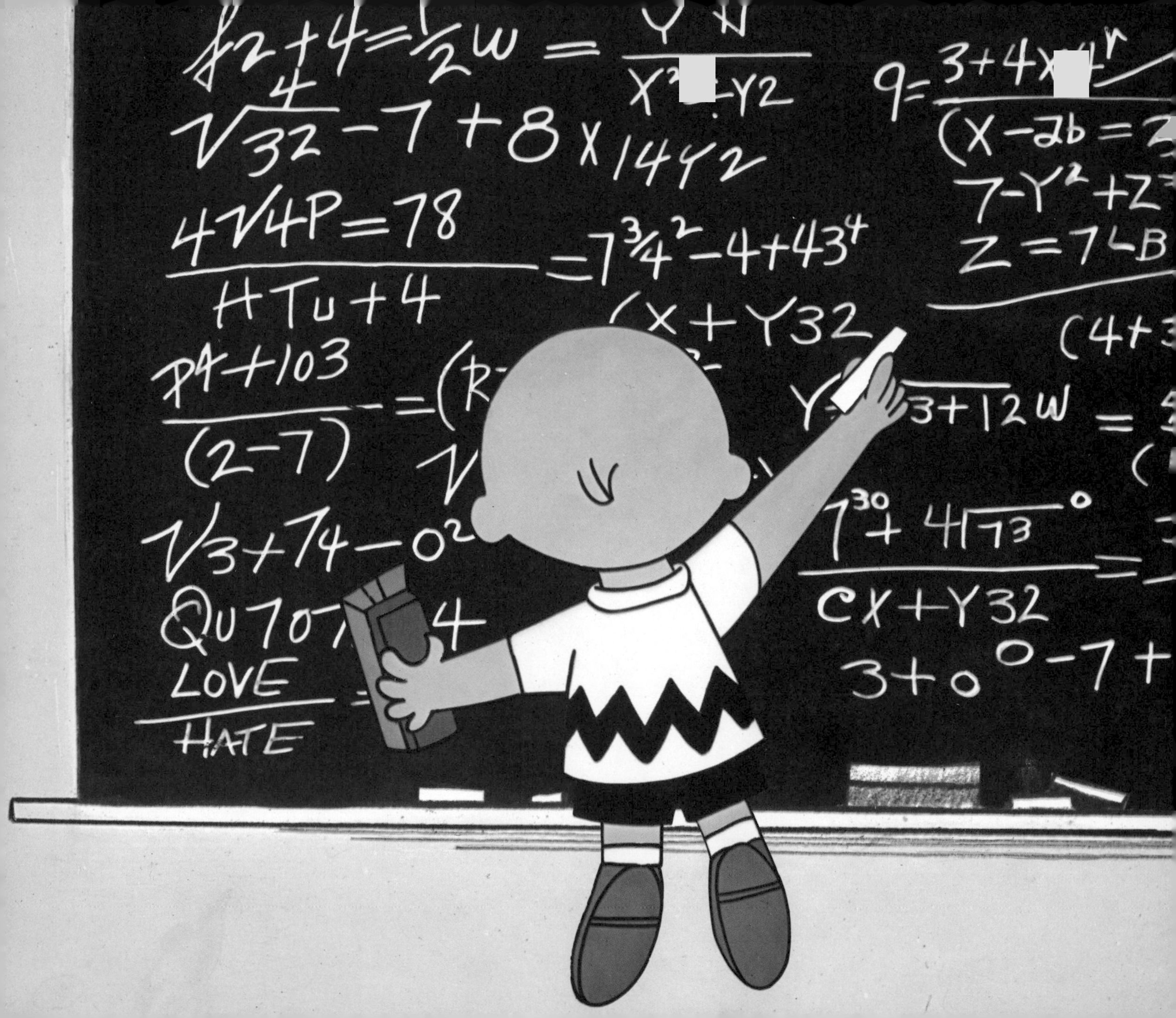

4V4P=78
HTu+4
P4+103
(2-7)
CX+Y32
LOVE
HATE

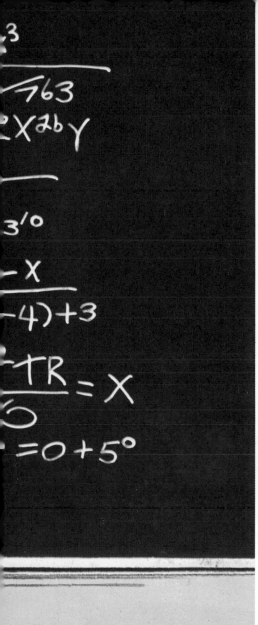

What a mass of figures! It looked like Charlie Brown was trying to solve all the math problems in the world at one time, so finally his teacher asked him if he knew what he was doing.

"No, ma'am, I don't have the slightest idea!"

For the second time in two days, the school room erupted with laughter aimed at poor ol' Charlie Brown. He was crushed.

He returned to his desk, and looked at the clock. The morning was about over. Soon the noon hour would be here, and school would be out, and summer vacation would begin, and the little red-haired girl would be gone. But why couldn't he be the first one out to the bus? Then he could stop her and quickly introduce himself, and tell her all the things he wanted to say. That was the answer! He looked at the clock again.

The minutes ticked away. Then the bell rang. Charlie Brown
leaped over his desk, and led the whole pack of shrieking children
in their mad race out of school.

He skidded to a stop and whirled to look for "his girl."

Kids swarmed all around him. He strained to catch a glimpse
of her. More kids ran by. He looked in all directions, but the crowd
was too much for him.

Before he knew what had happened, the bus doors closed and the huge vehicle pulled away.

Charlie Brown cried out in agony. Another failure. Another crushing blow. How could so many bad things happen to one person? Why couldn't something go right? Why did everything always have to turn out wrong? Why? Why did— What was this? What was this piece of paper in his hand? Someone had tucked a note into his hand!

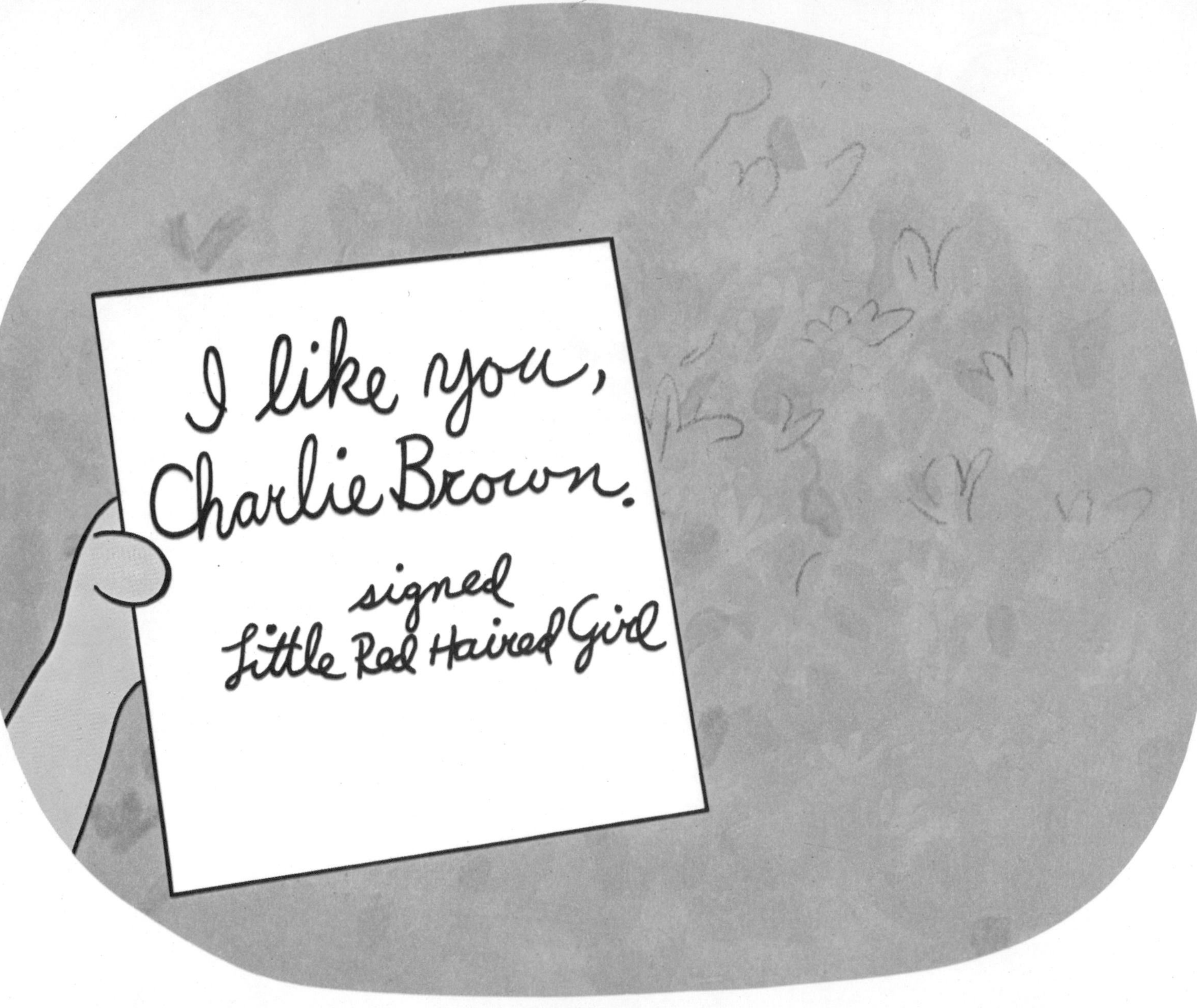
I like you, Charlie Brown.
signed
Little Red Haired Girl

Charlie Brown leaped into the air and danced all around the bus stop! He laughed and he shouted, and he jumped up and down, and he kicked his heels together, and he read the note again, and then he whirled in the air and danced around and around.

Then he went up the long hill toward home. Charlie Brown now had hope, and with his hope, he had love, for, after all, isn't that what love is all about?